THE FOLKLORE FILES

Warren Lane

dizzyemupublishing.com

DIZZY EMU PUBLISHING

1714 N McCadden Place, Hollywood, Los Angeles 90028

dizzyemupublishing.com

The Folklore Files
Warren Lane

First published in the United States
in 2022 by Dizzy Emu Publishing

dizzyemupublishing.com

THE FOLKLORE FILES

Warren Lane

FADE IN:

INT. HOOVER'S OFFICE BUILDING - SIXTH STORY - DAY

HOOVER JOHNSON (30), a Caucasian man in ill-fitting 1920s clothing, stands. His fedora hat is too small, his pin-striped suit is too big, and his wing-tip shoes are dull. Hoover excitedly grins, staring at a paper in his hand.

                    HOOVER
               (Southern twang)
          My stocks've done gone up! Way up!

SUPER: **BLACK TUESDAY, 1929**

                    DEUCE (O.S.)
               (Chicago accent)
          And here I am, Hoover.

Hoover looks across the room. DEUCE (30), Caucasian too, stands. He also sports 1920s clothing however his attire is fitting and slick--fedora hat, black suit, and shiny wing-tip shoes. There are things inhuman about him though--TINY HORNS protrude from his forehead and his eyes are completely BLACK.

                    DEUCE
          Wowza, ya can take da boy outta da
          backwoods but ya can't take da
          backwoods outta da boy. Dem new
          fancy city duds? Not you, Hoover.

                    HOOVER
          Here for my soul, Deuce?

                    DEUCE
          And how, your soul's gonna gimme da
          juice to start da Apocalypse.

                    HOOVER
          Apocalypse?

Suddenly a flapper-looking SECRETARY (30) opens a door.

                    FLAPPER SECRETARY
               (Betty Boopish)
          Your stocks crashed, Mista Johnson.
          Everybody's did. Folks are going
          apey out here. Hopefully it's all
          just baloney. We're still going to
          the juice joint tonight, right?

Hoover rushes over, slamming the door closed onto her.

                    DEUCE
          Hand over your soul.

                    HOOVER
          No, ya double-crossin' demon!

                    DEUCE
          I didn't double-cross you. Our deal
          was your soul in exchange for your
          stocks going up, dey went way up.

                    HOOVER
          But now they done crashed!

                    DEUCE
          Guess dat podunk family of yours
          ain't gonna be taken care of. No
          new house for Ma. No new baseball
          mit for Billy. No new nuttin'. Now
          hand over da soul, deal's a deal.

                    HOOVER
          No.

                    DEUCE
          But West-by-God-Virginia men are
          men of der word, am I right?

Hoover purses his lips.

                    DEUCE
          Well?

Hoover runs and dives through his office window CRASHING into

THE AIR, STORIES ABOVE WALL STREET - SAME

Six stories above Wall Street's main paved road and just
outside his office building, Hoover looks about--there are
several office buildings and several other Caucasian MEN in
suits also crashing forth from their office windows. Hoover
falls down until he hits the pavement in a bloody mess.

                                        BACK TO:

INT. HOOVER'S OFFICE - SAME

Deuce walks over to the shattered, gaping window. He looks
down on Hoover's bloody body resting atop the pavement.

                         DEUCE
                Aces, Apocalypse time.

                                        CUT TO BLACK

OVER BLACK...

SUPER: **3 YEARS LATER**

                         FDR (V.O.)
                    (staticky)
                "There is nothing to fear but fear
                itself, my New Deal will give jobs
                to millions of Americans..."

INT. JANE'S HOME OF SQUALOR - DAY

A dusty 1930s radio stands, the source of FDR's voice.

                         FDR (V.O.)
                "...so not to worry, we will get
                back onto our feet in no--"

A hand clicks off the radio. Reveal the owner's hand to be
JANE HOPE (25), African American. She stands before her
MOTHER (50), also African American. Both are dressed in
RAGGED CLOTHING. Their home is dusty, drab, and in ruins.

                         MOTHER
                We gonna up 'n sell that radio.

                         JANE
                But how're we gonna get the daily
                skinny if we do that, Ma?

                         MOTHER
                    (exploding)
                You backsassin' me, girl?!

Mother grabs a ROD and quickly raises it up, Jane cowers.
KNOCK-KNOCK--both look to their FRONT DOOR. Mother opens it.
Two FBI AGENTS (40s), both Caucasian men in suits, stand.

                         MOTHER
                May I help you, gentlemen?

                         FBI AGENT 1
                    (flashing a golden badge)
                We're here for Jane Hope, ma'am.

                         JANE
                I'm Jane Hope, sir.

Both FBI Agents step inside. FBI Agent 1 pulls a SILVER PEN
out from inside his jacket then he offers it to Jane.

                    JANE
          What's that?

                    FBI AGENT 1
          Your prize for winning the
          Presidential Poetry Contest.

                    FBI AGENT 2
          A solid silver pen, kid.

Jane takes it, staring at her solid-silver-prize-pen in awe.

                    MOTHER
          Tops, we can sell it.

                    JANE
          What?

                    MOTHER
          Get some money 'n fill our bellies.

                    FBI AGENT 1
          Selling the pen won't be necessary.

                    FBI AGENT 2
          Not necessary, ma'am.

                    MOTHER
          Lessen you gentlemen got some other
          way to fill my belly 'sides sellin'
          that silver pen, I'm sellin' it.

                    FBI AGENT 1
          We're also offering Jane a job on
          behalf of the president.

                    MOTHER
          What sorta job, gentlemen?

                    FBI AGENT 2
          Documenting folklore, ma'am.

                    MOTHER
          Huh?

                    FBI AGENT 1
          It's one of the jobs in the Federal
          Writers' Program under the New
          Deal, ma'am. Documenting folklore
          told by illiterate folks in
          America's backwooded regions.

                    FBI AGENT 2
          Documenting culture is important.

                    JANE
          FDR's sure got integrity.

                    FBI AGENT 1
          He sure does, kid, and the pay
          ain't nothin' to sneeze at neither.

                    MOTHER
          It's not, gentlemen?

                    FBI AGENT 2
          No, job pays well, ma'am.

                    FBI AGENT 1
          Very well, good thing you did such
          a great job with Jane, instilling
          your Christian values into her.

All look to a huge CROSS hanging on the wall.

                    MOTHER
          What does God have to do with this?

                    FBI AGENT 2
          Can't say, ma'am, classified.

                    FBI AGENT 1
          What my partner means to say is the
          Christian outlook in your
          daughter's poem really caught the
          president's eye. Touched his heart.

INT. FBI AGENT'S PARKED BLACK STUDEBAKER - MOMENTS LATER

FBI Agents 1 and 2 sit in the front seats. Jane sits in back.

                    JANE
               (super excited)
          Are we going to meet FDR now?!

                    FBI AGENT 1
          Let's get one thing straight, kid.
          FDR ain't in charge, his wife is.

                    JANE
          Eleanor Roosevelt?

                    FBI AGENT 2
          She pulls the strings behind the
          scenes, writes all of FDR's
          fireside chats you hear on the
          radio, came up with the New Deal to
          fix the economy, and figured out
          what's really going on in America.

                    JANE
          What's really going on in America?

                    FBI AGENT 1
          Evil, kid. Pure evil.

INT. HALLWAY JUST OUTSIDE THE OVAL OFFICE - LATER

Jane sits in a chair while the two FBI Agents loom over her.

                    FBI AGENT 1
          It'll be just a tick, kid.

                    FBI AGENT 2
          Yeah, the First Lady's in the Oval
          office with her main squeeze.

The FBI Agents point to the closed door which opens and
AMELIA EARHART (37) steps out. She has leather pilot goggles
resting atop her head and sports a white silk aviator scarf.

                    AMELIA
          Hiya, boys.

          FBI AGENT 1   FBI AGENT 2
          (saluting)   (saluting)
     Miss Earhart.   Miss Earhart.

                    JANE
          Amelia Earhart?! I'm a huge fan!

                    AMELIA
          Glad to hear it, kid.

                    ELEANOR (O.S.)
          Jane Hope, come!

All look to the still open oval office doorway.

                    AMELIA
               (to Jane)
          Oop, you're up, kid, and when the
          First Lady beckons, you don't wanna
          keep her waiting, believe you me.

                    (to FBI Agents)
          Buy me a whiskey, boys?

                    FBI AGENT 1
          If you tell us another story.

                    FBI AGENT 2
          What he means to say is of course
          we'll buy you a whiskey, ma'am.

                    AMELIA
          Off to the Monkey House then!

She locks arms with the FBI Agents. The trio heads off.

                    ELEANOR (O.S.)
          Jane Hope, I'm waiting!

Jane looks to the still open oval office doorway.

INT. OVAL OFFICE - SECONDS LATER

Jane sits. ELEANOR ROOSEVELT (50), thin, stands over her.

                    JANE
          Miss Earhart's your friend, ma'am?

                    ELEANOR
          And more.

                    JANE
          But what about your husband, ma'am?
                    (loud whispering)
          Does it not work cuz of the polio?

                    ELEANOR
          It works just fine. I like women is
          all, I am a lesbian. Franklin and I
          have an understanding. We do love
          each other in our way but enough
          about me, let's talk about you.

                    JANE
          One more question, if I may, ma'am.

                    ELEANOR
          Go on, ask your question.

                    JANE
          How come you run things, ma'am?

                    ELEANOR
          Franklin hates politics, always
          has. Fortunately, he loves me and I
          love politics so he let me use him
          in order for me to get involved.
          You see, I wrote the speeches that
          got him elected president. I didn't
          mean for them to be so impactful
          but they were and now here we are.

Eleanor holds up a poem entitled: *"Jesus Saves* by Jane Hope."

                    JANE
          Touched the president's heart,
          right, ma'am?

                    ELEANOR
          Franklin hasn't read it and frankly
          neither have I.

                    JANE
          Why am I here then?

                    ELEANOR
          Because evil will prevail as long
          as you do nothing, Jane Hope.

                    JANE
          Ma'am?

                    ELEANOR
          My spiritualist says we need you.
          Madam Zelda found you through
          psychometry. She touched your poem.
          That is why you are here. The
          Presidential Poetry Contest was a
          ruse to find, well, you. Madam
          Zelda touched every single one of
          the poems from the "contest" and
          when she touched yours the spirits
          revealed to her that you are the
          one. Our savior from the evil that
          is afoot. You see, a demon, he goes
          by the name of Deuce, has made
          several deals with backwoods folk
          and whenever a deal is done, you
          know, when it is time for whomever
          to pay up and hand over their
          promised soul, Deuce uses the
          powerful essence of said promised
          soul to break a seal.

                    JANE
          Seal?

                    ELEANOR
Of the Apocalypse of course. Deuce
has already broken the first seal,
well, third really.

                    JANE
Famine.

                    ELEANOR
Correct, famine. Revelation five--

                    JANE
Actually it's Revelation six, the
verse is five: "And when he opened
the third seal, I beheld a black
horse and he that sat on him had a
pair of balances in his hand."

                    ELEANOR
Wowza, was that just off the top?

                    JANE
But the bible's just a storybook.

                    ELEANOR
No, it is not and as I say, evil
will prevail as long as you do
nothing. I didn't believe it myself
until Madam Zelda showed me that
the storybook is real. Hang on a
tick, you have the bible memorized
but you don't believe it, Jane?

                    JANE
My Ma's made me read it every night
since my Daddy was lynched, lost my
faith on that Sunday ya might say.

                    ELEANOR
She *made* you read it?

                    JANE
Spare the rod, ya know?

                    ELEANOR
Still live with your mother, I see.

Eleanor nods to Jane's wrist--a bruise shows above the
sleeve. Jane pulls the sleeve up, covering her bruise.

                    ELEANOR
You must think I am cuckoo then if
you don't believe in any of this.

                    JANE
No, ma'am.

                    ELEANOR
Horsefeathers, you're placating me.
Are you not at least curious how
cuckoo I am? Ask me anything, Jane.

                    JANE
All right, in your story, why have
Deuce start with the third seal?

                    ELEANOR
The truth is we are not sure why
Deuce started with the third seal
but he did. If you doubt this,
simply look around--famine abounds.
We do however know that demons do
not traditionally handle souls.

                    JANE
They don't, ma'am?

                    ELEANOR
No, traditionally, the handling of
souls is reserved for much higher
beings, namely God and Satan, but
Deuce has and he has several more
deals lined up with backwoods folk.

                    JANE
Why is that significant?

                    ELEANOR
The essence of an innocent
backwoods soul is far more powerful
than the essence of a corrupt city
one. Also, backwoods folk are more
likely to pay-up when the time
comes. They take pride in being,
"men of their word." When Hoover
Johnson, yokel turned tycoon over
night, paid up his soul by jumping
out a Wall Street window three
years ago, it gave Deuce a great
bit of power, enough to break the
third seal. Madam Zelda says Hoover
Johnson's deal is the only
backwoods deal to come to fruition
thus far but Deuce has made
several. All about the wooded nukes
and crannies of this great country.

                    That is why I created and
                    incorporated the job of documenting
                    folklore told by backwoods folk
                    into the New Deal--the Federal
                    Writers' Program. It is a cover for
                    you and before you ask, yes you get
                    total authoritarian reign. That
                    means nowhere is off-limits for
                    you, "whites only" areas included.

She puts a golden badge into Jane's hand.

                         ELEANOR
              As I say, the spirits foretell you
              to be our savior from Deuce and his
              dealings so I'm putting you right
              into the thick of it. We have
              located where one of these deals is
              in the midst of fruition. That is
              to say, the human end is currently
              paying off but Deuce has not yet
              collected said human's soul. You
              must stop Deuce from getting that
              soul or he will break another seal.

                         JANE
              Will you house and feed my Ma?

                         ELEANOR
              If I agree will you take the job?

                         JANE
              Yes, ma'am.

                         ELEANOR
              Deal then.

Jane stands and they shake.

                         ELEANOR
              Don't worry, Madam Zelda is never
              wrong. Let's go meet your partner.

INT. DOME ARENA - FBI TRAINING CENTER - MOMENTS LATER

Boxing rings, gun galleries, and psychic testing areas fill
the enclosed dome. In the rings, men box. At the gun
galleries, men shoot. In the psychic testing areas, men quiz
one another via pictured cards. A cacophony of voices and
gunfire fill the place as Eleanor and Jane walk through it.

                    ELEANOR
          You are getting our best, trained
          by Elliot Ness. He is our number
          one across the board: the best
          pugilist, marksman, and psychic.

                    JANE
          What's his name, ma'am?

                    ELEANOR
          Special agent Jack Mulder and he is
          even from the backwoods of
          Tennessee. Your first mission. He
          knows the lingo and the people.
                    (pointing)
          There he is.

Jane looks to where Eleanor's pointing--TWO MEN are fencing
off to the side. Both wear white fencing uniforms, protective
dome-faced masks, and they brandish dull-tipped swords.

                    ELEANOR (O.S.)
          He fences during his free time, the
          chivalry of it all or some such.

One man lunges his sword into the red "heart" patch on his
opponent's chest, the sword bows. The winner quickly lowers
his sword and removes his dome-faced mask, revealing AGENT
JACK MULDER (30). He has blonde slicked down hair. He smiles.

                    ELEANOR
          Agent Mulder, come!

Jack jogs his way over towards Eleanor who looks to Jane.

                    ELEANOR
          Don't worry, he will protect you.

                    JANE
          I can take care of myself, ma'am.

                    ELEANOR
          He will be your guide then, yes?

Jane nods.

                    ELEANOR
          Great, Amelia will fly you both
          down to Tennessee tonight when she
          returns from the Monkey House.

INT. IN-FLIGHT CARGO-TYPE AIRPLANE - NIGHT

Amelia, flight goggles on now and whiskey bottle in hand, is
behind the flight-stick. Jane and Jack stand behind her.

                    AMELIA
          Took me an hour to crank this bird
          up but we'll be in Kentucky soon.

                    JACK
               (Southern twang)
          Kentucky? We's goin' to Tennessee.

                    AMELIA
          Right, that's what I meant.

Amelia looks about sheepishly for a moment then aggressively
jerks the flight-stick left causing the plane to mightily
shift. Jane and Jack fall to the floor--Jack atop Jane.

                    JANE
          Kindly get off of me, Agent Mulder.

Jack stands then helps Jane to her feet.

                    JACK
          Sorry, Agent Hope 'n you can just
          up 'n call me Jack by the by.

                    JANE
          You can just call me Jane.

                    JACK
          How come Eleanor pulled you, Jane?

                    JANE
          She believes I'm our "savior."

                    JACK
          From Deuce and his Apocalypse?

                    JANE
          You believe in all that stuff?

                    JACK
          'Course, don't you?

Jane shakes her head.

                    JACK
          Believe in God though, right?

                    JANE
          Not anymore.

                    JACK
How come?

                    JANE
After my Daddy and the rest of the
men in the congregation got lynched
one Sunday I lost my faith. I mean
if there's a God how could he let
that happen in his house on his
day? It doesn't make any sense.

                    JACK
If you don't believe in God or
nothin', why you here, Jane?

                    JANE
Made a deal with Eleanor, she
promised to look after my Ma.

                    JACK
Well, I hates my Ma, hates my whole
backwoods family. I hope you ain't
gonna take too much offense when
they treat you different 'n all.

                    JANE
Why would they do that?

                    JACK
On account of you bein' a negress.

                    JANE
Colored, please, I like *colored*.

                    JACK
Sorry, *colored*.

                    JANE
Is that why you hate your family so
much? Because they're prejudice?

                    JACK
Yup, even forbid me from marrying
the love of my life, Selma. I
respected they's wishes, family ya
know, so I didn't marry her. I
thought I'd fall out of love with
Selma someday but I didn't, it's
torture. Now I hates my family.

                    JANE
Is Selma colored like me?

                    JACK
          Cherokee 'n they hates injuns most.

EXT. JACK'S RAMSHACKLE FAMILY HOME - FRONT PORCH - SUNRISE

Jack and Jane stand on the ramshackle front porch before an
open front doorway. A sleepy-eyed, shirtless, suspender-
strapped, barefooted, JEREMIAH (35) stands in the door-frame.

                    JEREMIAH
               (Southern twang)
          That dumb injun done kilt herself.

Jack PUNCHES Jeremiah in the jaw, sending him reeling until
he falls down. PA (60), a bearded man in long-underwear, and
MA (60), a woman in a night-gown, appear in the door-frame.

                    MA
               (Southern twang)
          It's true, son.

                    PA
               (Southern twang)
          Suicide by pistol.

                    JACK
          What? Selma, why?

Jack begins blubbering as he crumbles to his knees. His
parents rush over and bend down. They hug-comfort Jack.

                    MA
          Sorry, son.

                    PA
          Sorry, boy, they already done
          buried her yesterdee.

In the background Jeremiah gets to his feet rubbing his jaw.

                    JEREMIAH
          That's it, baby Jack like y'all do,
          I'm the one done got a busted jaw.

                    JANE
          Put some ice on it, Jeremiah

All look to Jane who still stands on the porch.

                    JANE
          Sorry, I'm Jane, Jack's new
          partner, nice to meet you all.

                    JEREMIAH
          A lady negress?

                    JACK
               (still blubbering)
          Colored, Jeremiah, she likes
          colored 'n she's the first female
          agent we've had, the president hand-
          picked her hisself for the Federal
          Writers' Program in his New Deal.

                    PA
          Wowza, the first ever female agent--

                    MA
          --right here in our home.

                    JEREMIAH
          A negress agent that writes?

                    PA
               (exploding)
          Jeremiah, show Jack's new partner
          some galldang respect!

                    JEREMIAH
               (hanging his head)
          Sorry, Pa, I meant *colored*.

                    PA
          That's more like it, boy.
               (winking to Jane)
          Sorry, ma'am, somebody musta raised
          that boy wrong.

                    MA
          You sure did, Pa, so anyhow, Agent
          Jane, can I up 'n see you's badge?

Jane smiles while Jack continues to uncontrollably blubber.

EXT. CHEROKEE CEMETERY - DAY

A grave has been thrashed open. A TOMBSTONE lies beside it
that reads: "Selma Awiakta." A Cherokee family of three stand
looking down on the muddy mess in shock--CLYDE (30), his
wife, GERTRUDE (30), and their daughter, CINDY (7). Cindy
looks to a bouquet of colorful flowers in her hand. It's
bound together by a ROSARY. Cindy looks back up and smiles.

                    CINDY
          Uncle Jack!

Reveal that Jack and Jane approach over a hill. Cindy runs
over to Jack who quickly scoops her up in his arms.

                    JACK
          Miss me, Cindy?

                    CINDY
               (clearly hurt)
          Not really.

                    JACK
          Sorry I left without saying
          goodbye. You got the money, right?

                    CINDY
          Yup, found it in our old tree.

                    JACK
          I knew ya would.
               (nodding to her parents)
          Clyde. Gertrude.

          CLYDE   GERTRUDE
     (nodding back)   (nodding back)
Jack.   Jack.

Jack looks down to Selma's muddy thrashed open grave.

                    JACK
          What happened?

                    CLYDE
          We don't know.

                    GERTRUDE
          We just got here. Cindy wanted to
          put flowers on Selma's grave so we
          came out and found it like this.

                    CINDY
          Selma turned into a lycanthrope and
          tore herself out. The deal she made
          with Deuce. He wants my throne.

                    JACK
          What?

He looks to Cindy who's still in his arms.

                    CINDY
               (eyes turning BLACK)
          Deuce wants my thrown.

Jack sets her down and backs away until he's beside Jane.

                    JACK
          Who is you really?

Cindy drops her rosary bound bouquet.

                    CINDY
          I've gone by many names but you can
          just call me Satan, boy.

                    JACK
          The devil hisself?

                    CINDY
          In the flesh.

Cindy winks a black eye and flashes a grin.

                    JACK
          You's wrong about Selma, she would
          never make some deal with a demon.

                    CINDY
          She did though.

                    JACK
          No, Selma was too good.

                    CINDY
          That's why Deuce wants her soul.
          The essence of innocent souls is
          far more powerful than the essence
          of corrupt ones and Deuce needs all
          the muscle he can get to break all
          the seals and get all my demons.

                    JACK
          Get all your demons?

                    CINDY
          He already has half, if he starts
          the Apocalypse, he'll get the rest.
          Allegedly the Apocalypse is a real
          show stopper. Afterwards my demons
          will be so impressed that they'll
          help Deuce dethrown me and he'll
          take my place, I can't have that.
                    (looking to Jane)
          Daddy's down here by the by. He's
          been suffering in torment while
          your Ma beats you into reading that
          "holy" morality manual every night.

Cindy grins, her black eyes dazzling with delight. Unfazed,
Jane stares back her. Cindy frowns, disappointed.

                    CINDY
          Anyhoo, you're both wondering why
          Deuce broke the third seal first.
          The answer is cuz he doesn't know
          what he's doing. Apocalypse
          starting was only designed for me
          and God. Deuce is just a simp of a
          demon, oh sure he's gathering souls
          to have enough muscle to get the
          seals broken but he still doesn't
          have the know-how to do it right.

                    JACK
          I still don't get why Selma would
          make a deal in the first place.

                    CINDY
          Selma wanted revenge for the death
          of your love, dear boy. Selma knew
          she didn't have a mean enough
          constitution to do it proper, so
          she made a deal with Deuce to make
          everyone responsible pay for
          killing the love you shared. It
          started a few nights ago when the
          moon was full. The beast consumed
          her and family members against your
          love were slaughtered to death. Ya
          see, when Selma made the deal with
          Deuce, unbeknownst to her, he made
          her a lycanthrope. Clever, really.

                    JACK
          What's a lycanthrope?

                    CINDY
          A werewolf.

                    CLYDE (O.S.)
          It's true, Jack.

Jack looks to Clyde and Gertrude, both have shocked faces.

                    CLYDE
          Our family, animal attacks, hearts
          eaten right out of their chests.

                    GERTRUDE
          Past few nights on the Reservation.

                    CINDY
          See? Selma's getting her revenge.

                    JACK
          Why did she kill herself though?

                    CINDY
          Selma figured out what Deuce had
          turned her into. She kept waking up
          but never slept. Her lost moments
          of time lined up with the attacks.
          Selma shot herself to keep her
          family safe. Not a mean enough
          constitution. They buried her but
          when the moon rose again the beast
          came back. Selma turned, her fatal
          wound healed and she thrashed
          herself out. When the moon rises
          again tonight, she'll kill the last
          of her victims. The deal will be
          done and Deuce will come to collect
          her soul. Its essence will give him
          the power to break another seal.

                    JACK
          We's'll stop him before that.

                    CINDY
          Yes, by killing Selma before the
          deal is complete, silver is the
          only way to kill a lycanthrope.

                    JANE
          Hey, Cindy.

Cindy's black eyes dart over to Jane.

                    JANE
          In nomine dei, Lucifer, a nobis!

Cindy hisses then drops to the ground. Jack looks to Jane.

                    JACK
          What was that gobbledy-goop?

                    JANE
          Latin, learned it in my spare time.

Clyde and Gertrude rush to Cindy who sits up, eyes normal.

                    CINDY
               (looking about)
          What happened?

                    JANE
          You had a psychological episode.

                    CLYDE
          She had a what?

                    JANE
          You should get her mental help.

Clyde helps Cindy to her feet. The family walk over to their
1920s PICKUP, get inside, then drive off.

                    JACK
          If you don't believe Cindy was
          really the devil then why did you
          up 'n banish him with Latin?

                    JANE
          For Cindy's benefit.

                    JACK
          Huh?

Jane stares down at Cindy's rosary bound bouquet.

                    JANE
          Cindy's Christian, yes?

                    JACK
          The whole family converted a few
          years ago. A travelin' preacher
          come to town and got to 'em. So?

                    JANE
          I read about a case once, an
          exorcism. Halfway through the
          Catholic priest realized his
          subject wasn't truly possessed,
          just had psychological troubles but
          the priest still had to finish the
          exorcism because the subject, who
          was Christian by the by, believed
          it was real. So the priest used a
          Latin spoken banishment of the
          devil, it worked. Snapped the
          Christian out of his mental fit.

Jack turns, walking away.

                    JANE
          Where are you going?

                    JACK
              (over his shoulder)
          To prep my sword, the devil said
          only silver can kill a lycanthrope.

INT. BLACKSMITH SHOP - DAY

The BLACKSMITH (50), dirty and sweaty, holds a MEDIEVAL
looking SWORD in hand. He looks from the sword to Jack who
stands across the counter with Jane on the customer side.

                    BLACKSMITH
               (Southern twang)
          Lemme get this straight, boy, I
          made this here sword for you years
          ago to play King Arthur willy-nilly
          'n now you want me to coat the
          blade in silver just so's you all
          can admire it?

                    JACK
          That's right, Smitty.

Jack puts down a brick of silver and a stack of cash.

                    BLACKSMITH
          You's the boss, boy.

The Blacksmith picks up the silver brick and cash then he
rushes off, sword still in hand. Jane looks to Jack.

                    JANE
          This is daffy, Jack.

                    JACK
          You heard the devil, Jane.

                    JANE
          No, I heard a little girl who was
          play-acting like the "devil."

                    JACK
          Well, if I's wrong, then Selma
          won't show. No big deal, right?

EXT. CLYDE & GERTRUDE'S LOG HOME - FRONT PORCH - NIGHT

Jack, silver-coated sword in hand, and Jane both stand before
Clyde and Gertrude. Jack and Clyde are in an argument.

                    CLYDE
          Fine, Selma's a skinwalker out for
          revenge, Jack! But why would she
          come here?! I mean, we always
          supported your love together!

                    JACK
          Exactly, she'd come here for help!
          And PS, just because y'all didn't
          say nothin' against our love
          doesn't mean y'all are off the love-
          killin' hook! Y'all didn't say
          nothin' *for* our love neither!

Cindy, bouquet of flowers in hand, bursts forth from the
house. She immediately hands the bouquet to Jane.

                    CINDY
          That's for you.

Jane smells the flowers.

                    JANE
          Mmmm, thanks, Cindy.

                    CINDY
          You're welcome, Jane.

Gertrude looks down to Cindy.

                    GERTRUDE
          You should be in bed, missy.

                    CINDY
          So should you, Mom.

                    GERTRUDE
          You're right, let's go.

Gertrude and Cindy head inside. Clyde sighs, looking to Jack.

                    CLYDE
          Look, Jack, you can stay out here
          as long as you'd like tonight if it
          makes you feel better, there's
          plenty of moonlight for you both.

All look up to the FULL MOON when the sound of a branch
CRACKS causing them to look over at a DARK TREELINE.

                    JANE
          What was that?

                    CLYDE
             (sighing)
          My coyote troubles are never over.

                    JACK
          Check it out with me, Clyde.

SECONDS LATER

Jack, silver-coated sword still in hand, and Clyde approach
the DARK TREELINE. Jane watches from the front porch.

INT. DARK TREELINE - SAME

Jack and Clyde ENTER the dark treeline. They look about for a
moment when CRACK again. They look to a large tree. SELMA
AWIAKTA (30), Cherokee, steps out from around the trunk of
the tree. She wears a muddy shimmering flapper-type dress.

                    SELMA
          Jack?

Jack drops his silver-coated sword.

                    JACK
          Selma.

Jack rushes forth kissing Selma passionately.

                    JACK
          I missed you.

                    SELMA
          I missed you too, my love.

                    CLYDE
          I missed you too, cousin.

Selma looks to Clyde.

                    SELMA
          I didn't know where else to go.
               (voice turning demonic)
          Sorry, Clyde.

She pushes Jack down then SCREAMS, grabbing her head. She
drops to her knees as hair sprouts all over her body. Her
ears grow to points. Her face grows snoutish. Her eyes turn
yellow. Her teeth become fangs. She is now a snarling, teeth
gnashing, WEREWOLF. She quickly swipes, decapitating Clyde.

                    JACK
          No, Selma!

Jack crawls for his silver-coated sword but the werewolf
steps on it before Jack can grab it. He looks up to the
werewolf. It ROARS as it BACKHANDS Jack, sending him flying.

EXT. CLYDE & GERTRUDE'S LOG HOME - FRONT PORCH - SAME

Jane sits on the front porch, fiddling with her solid-silver-prize-pen when a ROAR sounds and Jack comes sailing out of the dark treeline. He lands in the yard. Jane looks to him.

                         JACK
               I dropped my sword.

The werewolf appears from the dark treeline. Jane tosses Jack her solid-silver-pen as the werewolf pounces. It lands on the pen, piercing its heart. It collapses atop Jack. It's dead.

                         DEUCE (O.S.)
               No!

Jack and Jane look to the dark treeline as Deuce steps out. Horns still protrude from his forehead and his eyes are still black. He angrily removes his hat, throwing it to the ground.

                         DEUCE
               You killed Selma before she could
               finish our deal! Before she could
               kill da remaining members of her
               love-killing family! Gertrude 'n
               lil' Cindy, it was gonna be my
               masterpiece! Da guilt woulda
               haunted Selma for all eternity down
               in Hell but you two ruined it!
                    (looking to the werewolf)
               Her soul's already gone up to
               heaven too! No chance of using it
               to break another seal! No chance!
               You'll pay for dis Jack 'n Jane!

Gertrude bursts out the front door of the house, brandishing a rosary in hand, cross forth. Deuce hisses then disappears, everyone faints and the dead werewolf bursts into flames.

                                             CUT TO BLACK

EXT. CLYDE & GERTRUDE'S LOG HOME - LATER

An unconscious Gertrude still lies in the yard. Jack too, now covered in ash. On the porch, Jane sits up, blinking her eyes open. She goes and stands over the limp ash-covered Jack.

                         JANE
               Jack?

He opens his eyes and sits up, rubbing his head.

                    JACK
          What happened?

                    JANE
          Deuce, must be some illusionist.

                    JACK
          He's a demon. Didn't you see his
          horns 'n black eyes 'n all?

                    JANE
          Ever heard of make-up?

                    JACK
          But--

                    JANE
          Jack, there's no such thing as
          demons, use your brain.

Jane helps Jack to his feet.

                    JACK
          What about everything we saw? Selma
          being a werewolf 'n all?

                    JANE
          Hypnosis.

Gertrude GROANS, still on the ground. Jane and Jack look down
to her. Cindy bursts out the front door and onto the porch.

                    CINDY
          Momma?!

Cindy rushes over and hugs Gertrude's neck as she sits up.

                    JANE (V.O.)
          Dear Eleanor...

INT. JACK'S RAMSHACKLE FAMILY HOME - DAY

Jane sits at a table writing a letter with her silver pen.

                    JANE (V.O.)
          We "interrupted" one of Deuce's
          "pacts" last night, not before
          someone lost his life though.

INT. BACKWOODS BAPTIST CHURCH - DAY

Full pews of BACKWOODS FOLK line both sides of a carpeted
aisle. At the end of the aisle is a closed COFFIN. Atop the
coffin is a PHOTO of Clyde. Cindy, Gertrude, and Jack stand
before the coffin. Cindy holds a bouquet bound by a rosary.

                    JANE (V.O.)
          I do not believe Deuce is a demon
          attempting to start the Apocalypse,
          however I do believe he is some
          sort of anarchist attempting to end
          this country and its families as we
          know them using smoke and mirrors.

Cindy puts her rosary bound bouquet atop Clyde's coffin.
Gertrude bursts into tears, Jack comforts her. Jeremiah, Ma,
and Pa rush to them from the front pew, hug-comforting them.

                    JANE (V.O.)
          Jack and I will not let Deuce win.

                                        BACK TO:

INT. JACK'S RAMSHACKLE FAMILY HOME - DAY

Jane continues to pen her note at the table.

                    JANE (V.O.)
          Deuce uses illusions to instill
          fear into devout people. Deuce's
          motive is mass hysteria which will
          consume this nation. Gertrude
          identified him as the preacher who
          came through town three years ago.
          Clearly a ruse to convert as many
          "souls" as he can--make them
          believers then control them with
          superstition. Whomever is right
          about Deuce. Me? You? No matter,
          our goal is the same: stop Deuce.

INT. OVAL OFFICE - DAY

Reveal Eleanor sitting as she silently reads Jane's letter.

                    JANE (V.O.)
          I understand what you meant now.
          Evil indeed prevails as long as I
          do nothing, well, Jack and I want
          to keep doing something. We await
          our next assignment. Yours, Jane.

Eleanor nods, having finished the letter, then she slides it into a manila folder labeled: "The Folklore Files."

INT. DIMLY LIT ROOM - SAME MOMENT

At a round table sits Amelia, the wheelchair bound FDR (50), and a woman wearing a black veil. This is MADAM ZELDA (70s). Her elderly fingers impatiently drum atop the round table.

                    FDR
          Apologies, Madam Zelda, but Ellie
          should be here any minute.

The door of the room opens and Eleanor steps inside.

                    ELEANOR
          Sorry, I'm late, I just finished
          reading Jane's letter. She's in.

Eleanor quickly goes to the table, kisses FDR and Amelia on their cheeks, then she sits between them. Eleanor then hands "The Folklore Files" folder over to Madam Zelda who promptly opens it and touches Jane's letter. Madam Zelda jolts to.

                    ELEANOR
          What do the spirits reveal to you
          about Jane this time, Madam Zelda?

                    MADAM ZELDA
               (lifting her veil)
          The spirit of Jane Hope's father
          has shown me that her next
          confrontation with Deuce will take
          place deep within the witch
          infested swamps of Louisiana.

FDR and Eleanor look to Amelia who sighs.

                    AMELIA
          I know, I'm goin', I'm goin' but if
          it takes me an hour to crank up
          that bird again, I'm out.
               (standing)
          Louisiana's under Arkansas, right?

                                        FADE OUT.